P9-DNP-495

THIS IS FALCON

Written by **Clarissa Wong**

Illustrated by **Ron Lim** *and* **Rachelle Rosenberg**

Based on the Marvel comic book series **The Avengers**

Los Angeles
New York

marvelkids.com

© 2015 MARVEL

Printed in the United States of America
First Edition, February 2015
1 3 5 7 9 10 8 6 4 2
G658-7729-4-14360
ISBN 978-1-4847-2259-6

SUSTAINABLE FORESTRY INITIATIVE

Certified Chain of Custody
Promoting Sustainable Forestry

www.sfiprogram.org
SFI-01415

The SFI label applies to the text stock

Sam Wilson likes birds.
His favorite bird is the falcon.
Sam lives in New York City.

Sam tries to do what is right.
But sometimes
this gets him into trouble.

He has a pet bird.
It is a falcon named Redwing.
They fight crimes together.

Sam wants to be an Avenger.
His favorite hero is
Captain America.

One day, Sam and Redwing
get into trouble.
The crooks chase after them.

Sam and Redwing fight back.
But the crooks outnumber them!

It's a good thing Captain America
jumps in! Cap saves the day!

Sam cannot believe it!
Captain America is his idol.

Captain America sees Sam as
a good fighter.
He agrees to mentor Sam at S.H.I.E.L.D.
Sam becomes known as Falcon!

Falcon puts on wings.
He must learn to fly.

Sam tries his best.
It is not always easy.

But he wants to help people.

He wants to be a hero.

Now Sam can fly in the sky.
He can fly like a bird.

Falcon can fly up.

Falcon can swoop down.

He can perch in a tree.

Falcon can kick in midair.

Redwing goes
wherever Falcon goes.
They fly together.

Falcon can fight in the sky.

Falcon can fight on land.

Falcon is a great fighter.
Captain America
is impressed.

Captain America and Falcon are friends.
Captain America wants Falcon
to be his fighting partner.

They take on the bad guys.
They fight as a team.

Captain America battles villains on land.
Falcon charges at the villains from
the sky.

Falcon meets another S.H.I.E.L.D. agent. Her name is Black Widow. She is an Avenger, too.

Sam fights with Cap and Black Widow.
They are a great team.

Sam wants to prove he is a Super Hero.
He is ready.

Nick Fury likes Sam.

He knows Sam works hard.

He thinks Sam can help.

Falcon meets all the Avengers.
Everyone gets along.

The Avengers want Falcon
to be part of their team!
Falcon is now an Avenger!